Cassell Publishers Limited
Wellington House
125 Strand
London
WC2R OBB

Nursery Rhymes of London Town
first published 1916

More Nursery Rhymes of London Town
first published 1917

Complete Edition first published 1938
by Gerald Duckworth and Co. Ltd

This fascimile edition published 1996

British Library Cataloguing in Publication Data
A catalogue record for this book is available from the British Library

ISBN 0-304-34899-6

Printed and bound in Great Britain by Hillman Printers Ltd

Contents

Contents

Contents

Contents

SEVERAL of these verses originally appeared in *Punch* and the author is indebted to the proprietors of that journal for permission to republish them in book form.

WEST END LANE

JOAN was born in West End Lane,
  And when she was born she was young;
Joan was born on a Monday morn
  While the nine-o'clock bell was rung;
And if little Joan had never been born
  These songs would have never been sung.

Kingsway

WALKING on the King's Way, lady my lady,
    Walking on the King's Way will you
    go in red?
With a silken wimple and a ruby on your finger,
And a furry mantle trailing where you tread?

Neither red nor ruby I'll wear upon the King's
    Way,
I will go in duffle grey with nothing on my head.

Walking on the King's Way, lady my lady,
Walking on the King's Way will you go in blue?
With an ermine border, and a plume of peacock
    feathers,
And a silver circlet, and a sapphire on your shoe?

Neither blue nor sapphire I'll wear upon the
    King's Way,
I will go in duffle grey and barefoot too.

Walking on the King's Way, lady my lady,
Walking on the King's Way will you go in
    green?
With a golden girdle, and a pointed velvet
    slipper,
And a crown of emeralds fit for a queen?

Neither green nor emerald I'll wear upon the
King's Way,
I will go in duffle grey so lovely to be seen,
And the King will stop and kiss me and call me
his Queen.

The Spaniards

THREE Spaniards dwell on Hampstead Heath:
　　One has a Scowl and a Knife in a Sheath,
One twangs a Guitar in the bright Moonlight,
One chases a Bull round a Bush all Night!

Mayfair

WILL you go along with me to Shepherd
      Market?
  It's there they hold the merriest Fair in May.
Will you go along with me to Shepherd Market
  In a pair of red-heeled slippers very gay?
I'll pick a bunch of cowslips for your bodice,
  And I'll tie a yellow ribbon in your hair,
If you'll go along with me to Shepherd Market
  And dance me round the Maypole at May-Fair.

Piccadilly

PICK a dilly ; pick a daffy ! pick a daffy-dilly !
    The flower-girls at the fountain-head are
        nodding willy-nilly—
Quick ! before they wake again, slip among 'em,
    will ye?
And pick a dilly, pick a daffy, pick a daffy-dilly !

King's Cross

King's Cross!
    What shall we do?
His Purple Robe
Is rent in two!
Out of his Crown
He's torn the gems!
He's thrown his Sceptre

Into the Thames!
The Court is shaking
In its shoe —
King's Cross!
What shall we do?
Leave him alone
For a minute or two.

Bishopsgate

BISHOPSGATE Without!
   Bishopsgate Within!
What a clamour at the Gate,
   O what a din!
Inside and Outside
The Bishops bang and shout,
Outside crying, "Let me In!"
Inside, "Let me Out!"

Blackfriars

SEVEN Black Friars sitting back to back
Fished from the bridge for a pike or a jack.
The first caught a tiddler, the second caught a
crab,
The third caught a winkle, the fourth caught a
dab,
The fifth caught a tadpole, the sixth caught an
eel,
And the seventh one caught an old cart-wheel.

Clement and Clifford

CLEMENT and Clifford do not roam,
    When you call they're always Home—
"Yes," says the Maid who lifts the pin,
"Clement's In and Clifford's In."

Highgate

ON the Hill there stands a Gate
  Where folk go early and come back late.
The young ones leap to reach the crown
And meet the old ones limping down.
Their tongues are mute and their eyes are wide,
And they tell no tales of the other side.
None who has been there ever will
Speak of the High Gate on the Hill.

The Stock Exchange

THERE'S a Bull and a Bear, and what do you
  think?
They live in a Garden of white Stocks and pink.
"I'll give you a pink Stock for one of your
  white,"
Says the Bear to the Bull, and the Bull says,
  "All right!"
They never make answer if any one knocks,
They are always so busy exchanging their Stocks.

The Poultry and the Borough

THE Fox ran to London
    Starving for his dinner,
There he met the Weasel
    Looking even thinner.

The Weasel said to Reynard,
    "What shall be our pickings?"
Said Reynard to the Weasel,
    "Rabbits and Spring Chickens."

Then they went a-hunting
    And they did it very thorough,
The Fox in the Poultry
    And the Weasel in the Borough.

Shepherd's Bush

O IF you go to London Town you'll find a
  Shepherd there
Who sits beneath a Hawthorn Bush and pipes a
  sylvan air ;
And little bleating kids and woolly lambkins
  crowd and push
To dance and prance of a May Morning around
  the Shepherd's Bush.

Seven Sisters, Sevenoaks, Seven Kings and Seven Dials

SEVEN Sisters in patchwork cloaks
    Sat in the shadow of Seven Oaks
Stringing acorns on silken strings,
Awaiting the coming of Seven Kings.

Seven years they endured their trials
And then they consulted their Seven Dials—
"O it's time, it's time, it's time," they said,
"It's very high time that we were wed!"

Tally-Ho Corner, Etc.

TALLY-HO! Tally-ho! Tally-ho!
  We unearthed the old Vixen in Bow,
   Her trail in the dark
   We lost in Hyde Park
To the windward of Rotten Row,
But we found it again in Soho, so-ho!
   The Hunt did hollow,
   The Hounds did bell,
   Holloway, holloway,
   Follow the call away,
After her, after her, lads, Pell-mell!
  Tally-ho! Tally-ho! Tally-ho!
  Which way did the Vixen go?
   Without a warner
   She ran round the Corner
Where a Jew was calling, "Old Clo', Old clo'!"
   She crossed his scent
   With cunning intent,
  And *didn't* the Vixen crow
When off to the Jewry the pack went past of her!
At Tally-ho Corner the Hunt saw the last of her:
   Ho! Tally-ho! Tally-ho!

Old Ford

OLD Ford, Old Ford, he lives by himself
   Because he lives alone.
His roof is straw, his bed a shelf,
   His breakfast is a bone,
A broken groat is the whole of his pelf
   And he keeps it under a stone.

Smithfield and Houndsditch

THERE was a Smith lived in a Field,
　　　He was as strong as any,
An Iron hammer he did wield
　　And his fee was a silver penny.
The travelling merchants with their bags
　　In long processions trod,
And to the Smith-Field brought their nags
　　To get them newly shod.

He had a Hound lived in a Ditch,
　　It had a ragged ear,
Two eyes like coals and a coat like pitch;
　　He held his good Hound dear.
Its scent was quick for friend or foe,
　　And when they heard it bark
The Villains never liked to go
　　By the Hound's-Ditch in the dark!

Battersea

Little boy, little boy, what is the matter?—
  Madam, the sea has been turned into
    batter!

Little boy, little boy, what does it matter?—
Madam, I cannot go swimming in batter.

Little boy, little boy, that's no great matter!—
Madam, how *shall* I get rid of the batter?

Why, with your spoon and your fork and your
    platter, see,
Little boy, little boy, eat up the Batter-Sea!

Limehouse and Poplar

I PLANTED a limestone once upon a time,
And up came a little wee House of Lime.

I planted a seed by the
corner of the wall,
And up came a Poplar
ninety feet tall.

I settled down for life, as
happy as could be,
In my little wee Lime-
House by my big
Poplar-tree.

Knightsbridge

COME up, come up to London Town! it's full
    of charming sights!
For instance, there's a Bridge that's used by
    nobody but Knights.
With shining lance and coat of mail they clank
    it up and down,
And hold tournaments on Knightsbridge in the
    heart of London Town.

A COACH-AND-SIX TO CHELSEA

Orchard Street

THE fruit hangs ripe, the fruit hangs sweet,
    High and low in my Orchard Street,
Apples and pears, cherries and plums,
Something for every one who comes.
    If you're a Pedlar
    I'll give you a medlar,
    If you're a Prince
    I'll give you a quince,
    If you're a Queen
    A nectarine,
    If you're the King
    Take anything,
Apricots, mulberries, melons, or red and white
Currants like rubies and pearls on a string!
    Little girls each
    Shall have a peach,
Boys shall have grapes that hang just out of
    reach—
Nothing's to pay, whatever you eat
Of the fruit that grows in my Orchard Street.

London Wall

A ROMAN built up London Wall,
  With his big bricks and his little bricks,
A Roman built up London Wall
With its straw and its lime and its mortar and all.

Then he stood on the top, so stalwart and tall,
  On the big bricks and the little bricks,
He stood on the top so stalwart and tall,
With his spear and his shield and his helmet and
    all.

He looked down on London, all bustle and brawl
  And big bricks and little bricks,
He looked down on London, all bustle and brawl,
With its streets and its chimneys and markets
    and all.

With its mansions, its rivers, its parks and
    Whitehall,
  And its big bricks and its little bricks,
With its mansions, its rivers, its parks and
    Whitehall,
Its prisons, its churches, its Tower and St. Paul.

"I've built up a Wall that never can fall,
   With my big bricks and my little bricks,
I've built up a Wall that never can fall
By cannon, or thunder, or earthquake and all!"

But London laughed low and began for to crawl
   Through the big bricks and the little bricks,
London laughed low and began for to crawl
To the North, to the West, to the
      South, East and all.

There came a great crack in the
      side of the Wall,
   In the big bricks and the little
      bricks,
There came a great crack in the
      side of the Wall,
And down fell the Wall and the
      Roman and all!

Whitechapel

THE little White Chapel is ringing its bell
    With a ring-a-ding-dong,
    All day long
But what it is ringing for no one can tell—
    And that's my song
    With a ring-a-ding-dong!

St. John's Wood

Saint John walked in a Wood
  Where elm-trees spread their branches,
And squirrels climbed and pigeons cooed
And hares sat on their haunches.
He built him willow huts
Wherever he might settle,
His meat was chiefly hazel-nuts,
His drink the honey nettle.
His Wood that grew so green
Is now as grey as stone ;
His Wood may any day be seen,
But where's the good Saint John ?

Hammersmith

Hammer, Smith! hammer, Smith!
   What will you shoe my pony with?
      I'll shoe it with a shoe of steel,
      Another of gold so red,
      A third shoe of ivory,
      And a fourth shoe of lead.
Then I'll pay you with a brass farthing
I picked up out of the roadway,
So hammer, Smith! hammer, Smith!
For I want to ride down the Broadway.

Cheapside

THINGS are Cheap this side, things are **Dear**
on that—
I shall shop on the Cheap-Side when I buy my
Holiday Hat!

Kensal Rise

KENSAL is a Sleepy-head—
    Run and pull her out of bed!
Five o'clock and six are gone,
Lazy Kensal slumbers on;
Seven has struck and eight is past,
Kensal still is snoring fast,
While her angry Mistress cries:
"Get up, Kensal! Kensal, rise!"

Parson's Green

I N a Village where I've been
    They keep their Parson on a Green.
They tie him to a Juniper Tree
And bring him Currant Bread for tea.
A jollier man I've never seen
Than the one on Parson's Green.

Threadneedle Street

THERE is an Old Lady in Threadneedle Street
  Sits threading of needles so deft and so
    neat.
"Come bring me your needles, young girls, if
    you've any,
I'll thread you a gross for the price of a Penny.
If you only bring one it will cost you a Brown,
But I'll thread all the needles in town for a
    Crown!"

Swiss Cottage

I HEARD a Jodeller
   In a Swiss Cottage
Eating a crust
And a bowl of hot pottage.

He jodelled and jodelled
'Twixt every bite,
He jodelled until
Not a crumb was in sight!

He jodelled and jodelled
'Twixt every sup,
He jodelled until
He had drunk it all up!

He put down his bowl
And he came to the door,
And jodelled and jodelled
And jodelled for more!

The Bank

THERE'S a Bank, a pretty Bank, blooming
without stint—
What does it bloom with? Gold and Silver Mint.
The Silver is for Noblemen, the Gold is for the
King,
And there's Copper for the Commoners who go
a-gathering.

Leadenhall

A KING who is dead
        Had a Hall made of Lead
That contained neither window nor door;
    When they built the last wall
    Of the King's Leaden Hall
He never was seen any more.

The Strand

THE loveliest maidens in the land,
    Girls in rags and ladies grand,
All go wandering down the Strand,
    Ding, dong, ding!
To look for pearls in oyster-shells
And listen to Saint Martin's bells,
    Ding, dong, ding!

Some get amber, some get jet,
Silver fish-scales others get
In a golden fishing-net,
    Ding, dong, ding!
Some find crowns of seaweed there
And flowers of coral for their hair,
    Ding, dong, ding!

All day long they have delight,
Then the Thames flows in at night
And sweeps the maidens out of sight,
    Ding, dong, ding!

Down the Strand their lovely knells
Echo from Saint Martin's bells,
    Ding, dong, ding!
    Ding, dong, ding!

Waterloo

WATER, Loo! water, Loo! fetch me some
water!
There isn't a drop for a mile and a quarter!
The ground is so hard and the ground is so dry
I'm frightened my little red rose-bush will die.

Water, Loo! water, Loo; fetch me some water!
My little red rose-bush grows shorter and shorter!
It wants but a pitcherful, then it will flower
And grow in an instant as tall as the Tower.

Pimlico

PIMLICO, pamlico, pumpkins and peas!
    Pepper them properly, else you will sneeze,
Pop in a pipkin and leave them till one,
Pimlico, pamlico, then they'll be done!

Shepherdess Walk

WALK, Shepherdess, walk,
 And I'll walk too,
To find the ram with the ebony horn
And the gold-footed ewe;

The lamb with the fleece of silver
Like summer sea-foam,
And the wether with the crystal bell
That leads them all home.

Walk, Shepherdess, walk,
And I'll walk too,
And if we never find them
I shan't mind, shall you?

Ladywell

THE Lady sat
 On the brink of the Well,
She lost her balance
And in she fell!
They fished her up
With a crooked pin,
She came out wetter
Than she went in.

Well, Lady, well!
Sir, very ill!
If you sit by the Well
You are certain to spill.

Haymarket

I WENT up to the Hay-market upon a summer's
day,
I went up to the Hay-market to sell a load of hay,
To sell a load of hay and a little bit over,
And I sold it all to a pretty girl for a nosegay of
red clover.

A nosegay of red clover and a hollow golden
straw,
Now wasn't that a bargain, the best you ever saw?
I whistled on my straw in the market-place all
day,
And the London folk came flocking for to foot
it in the hay.

Primrose Hill

PRIMROSE Hill is green,
    Primrose Hill is yellow.
As I walked on Primrose Hill
I met a pretty fellow.
We went up the Hill,
We went down the Valley,
We went through the Primroses
And he said, "Will you marry?"

He gave me a silver clasp
And a golden ring.
We sat in the Primroses
And heard the thrushes sing.
The month it was April,
The day it was sunny,
I plucked him a Primrose
And the moon came up like honey.

The Angel

THE Angel flew down
    One morning to town
But didn't know where to rest,
For they shut her out of the East End
And they shut her out of the West.

    The Angel went on
    To Islington,
And there the people were kinder.
If ever you go to Islington
That's where you will find her.

Brook Green

Brook green, green brook, whither do you
    run?
Down to Fulham Palace to shine in the sun.
Whom will you see there? Seventeen Princesses
Who come in the morning to pick my water-
    cresses.

Billingsgate

TROT, mare, trot, or I'll be late,
And Billing will have locked his Gate

Mister Billing,
Are you willing
To open your Gate to me?
Yes! says Billing,
Give me a shilling
And I will fetch the key.

Mister Billing,
I haven't a shilling,
I'll give you a button of horn.
No! says Billing,
I'm unwilling,
A button will buy no corn.

Take it or leave it, but I can't wait—
Jump, mare, jump over Billing's Gate!

Fleet Street

IN Fleet Street, in Fleet Street, the People are
   so fleet
They barely touch the cobble-stones with their
   nimble feet!
The Lads run like a windy day, the Lasses run
   like rain,
From Temple Bar to Ludgate Hill, and then run
   back again.

Wormwood Scrubs

Wormwood scrubs, Wormwood scrubs
  Windows, walls, and floors,
Pots and pans and pickle-tubs,
  Tables, chairs and doors;
Wormwood scrubs the public seats
  And the City Halls,
Wormwood scrubs the London streets,
  Wormwood scrubs Saint Paul's.
Wormwood scrubs on her hands and knees,
  But oh, it's plainly seen
Though she use a ton of elbow-grease
  She'll *never* get it clean!

Petticoat Lane

Up the Lane and down the Lane and all round
    about
The Petticoats on Washing-day are all hanging
    out;
Some are made of linsey-woolsey, some are made
    of silk,
Some of them are green as grass and some are
    white as milk.
Frilled and flounced and quilted ones in Petticoat
    Lane,
Some are worked in coloured nosegays, some of
    them are plain,
Some are striped with red and blue as gaudy as
    can be,
And one is sprigged with Lavender, and that's
    the one for me.

Temple Gardens

IN the Temple Gardens
   On an April day
The palm on the Embankment
Is gold instead of grey.

Out of the Temple
Run the boys and girls
Dressed in smocks of linen
With garlands on their curls.

Some are gay and joyful,
Some are proud and calm,
They go down to the water
And gather wands of palm.

Round the Temple Gardens
They shake their branches bright,
And the bloomy catkins tumble
Like balls of yellow light.

Chalk Farm

SOME farmers farm in fruit, some farm in grain,
　　Others farm in dairy-stuff, and many farm
　　　　in vain,
But I know a place for a Sunday morning's walk
Where the Farmer and his Family only farm in
　　chalk.
The Farmer and his Family before you walk back
Will bid you in to sit awhile and share their mid-
　　day snack—
O they that live in Chalk Farm they live at their
　　ease,
For the Farmer and his Family can't tell chalk
　　from cheese.

Oxford Circus

THE Circus has come from Oxford City
    With Ponies and Jugglers and Ladies so
        pretty.
Pay up your pennies and don't be shirkers—
All the Fun of the Fair is at Oxford Circus!

Peckham Rye

"Who'll buy our Rye?
Who'll buy? who'll buy'
The pretty girls of Peckham cry :
"The ears are full as they can hold
And heavy as a purse of gold.
Sweeter corn you will not find
For the London mills to grind—
Come buy, come buy
Our Peckham Rye!"

Glasshouse Street

DON'T throw stones in Glasshouse Street,
     in Glasshouse Street,
     in Glasshouse Street,
Don't throw stones in Glasshouse Street,
     Or you'll—be—beat!

Two small boys in Glasshouse Street
One March morning happened to meet—
    A stone flashed,
    A window smashed,
    A chimney-pot
            crashed,
    And the boys were
    thrashed!

So *don't* throw stones in
    Glasshouse Street,
    in Glasshouse Street,
    in Glasshouse Street,
Don't throw stones in
    Glasshouse Street
    Whoever — you —
    meet!

Longacre and Broad Street

IT's odds that I wouldn't be singing this song
    If the Acre were only as broad as it's long,
And if only the Street were as long as it's broad
The song I am singing would go by the board.
But Longacre's thin as the slip of the moon,
And Broad Street is short as my slip of a tune.

Afterword

(For J. T.)

LONDON THORP

I KNOW a thorp, a pleasant thorp,
Not found on Weald or Down,
That flourishes beside the Thames
South-West of London Town.

One day with fifty simple rhymes
I thither did repair,
And my songs and I were welcomed by
The only native there.

Now Heaven bless that pleasant thorp
Which treated us so kind!
North-West, North-West the singer goes,
But leaves her songs behind.

For kindness makes a thing its own,
In ways time cannot warp—
These songs are thine as much as mine,
And thankee, J-s-ph Th-rp.

ENGLAND'S LANE

UP the Lane of England,
  Where the babies grow,
With a pack of nursery rhymes
  Peddling I go.
I'm looking for a little girl
  For to sing my songs to,
I'm looking for the little girl
  My pack of songs belongs to.
She came in a snow-storm
  One January day,
She sheltered in a trim grove
  And there she did stay;
Her pretty name is Joscelyn,
  She wears a fine gold chain—
Has any one seen Joscelyn
  Who grows in England's Lane?

Whitehall

CHILDREN, children, cheat the dawn
  And pick the daisies on the lawn,
Pick them while the dew is on
  And carry them into the White Hall.
The Bride is waiting for her boy,
Kiss her slippers and wish her joy,
Scatter your daisies under her feet
  And sing and dance in the White Hall.

Maids, maids, to the garden go
And gather the lilies pure as snow
Until your aprons overflow,
  And carry them into the White Hall.
The Bride is waiting for her boy,
Kiss her hands and wish her joy,
Put your lilies in her arms
  And sing and dance in the White Hall.

Wives, wives, go down to the bower
And break a branch of orange-flower,
Make a wreath within the hour
  And carry it into the White Hall.
The Bride is waiting for her boy,
Kiss her brow and wish her joy,
Place your wreath upon her head
  And sing and dance in the White Hall.

Groom, groom, go into the grove
And find a rose as white as a dove,
Find another as red as love
    And carry them into the White Hall.
The Bride is waiting for her boy,
Kiss her lips and wish her joy,
Lay your roses on her heart
    And wed your Bride in the White Hall.

St. Martin's-in-the-Fields

Saint Martin's in the Fields,
Saint Martin's in the Fields,
Considering the Barley
To find what it yields;
If the yield is scanty
He's going to plant Oats
And sell the crop for Lamb's-wool
To make Beggars Coats.

Bloomsbury

BLOOMSBURYING! bloomsburying!
    Who will go a-bloomsburying?
Down, down, with a derry-down-derrying,
Who will go a-bloomsburying?
        Shovels and spades
        And birchen brooms,
        Summer is dead
        With all her blooms!
        Who will her blooms bury?
        You and I.
        Cover them up
        Where they do lie.
Bloomsburying! bloomsburying!
We must go a-bloomsburying.
Down, down, with a derry-down-derrying,
We'll all go a-bloomsburying.

Nine Elms

NINE Elms in a ring :
  In One I saw a Robin Swing,
In Two a Peacock spread his tail,
In Three I heard the Nightingale,
In Four a White Owl hid with craft,
In Five a Green Woodpecker laughed,
In Six a Ring-Dove croodled low,
In Seven lived a quarrelling Crow,
In Eight a million Starlings flew,
In Nine a Cuckoo said, Cuckoo !

Earl's Court and Baron's Court

EARLS court
With knee bent low,
Barons court
With a kiss and a blow.
I dropped a curtsey to the Earl,
I'm the Baron's lady-O!

Rushy Green

THE banks are rushy green,
   The banks are rushy green,
And steep enough and deep enough to hide a
      Runaway Queen!
   Hang your crown on a rush,
   Hide your shoes in the brush,
Paddle your feet in the water sweet, you never
      will be seen.
   The banks are rushy green,
   The banks are rushy green,
Put your crown and slippers on, and don't say
      where you've been.

Child's Hill

O<small>N</small> the Child's Hill
  I saw the Child
Laughing his fill
And running wild.

"Child, come home!
It is time to sup."
"I will not come
Till the moon is up."

Up she popped
Like a ball of flame,
And down she dropped
When morning came.

The Child ran in
From his Hill so green,
And said, "I have seen
What I have seen!"

Nunhead

I saw a little Nun-head peeping through the
bars.
"What are you doing, Nun?" "Telling the
stars.
The Twins and the Fishes, the Virgin and the
Wain,
I'm telling them all like the beads on my chain."

Bayswater

THE Bays came down to water—
    Neigh! neigh! neigh!
And there they found the Brindled Mules—
    Bray! bray! bray!
"How dare you muddy the Bays' water
    That was as clear as glass?
How dare you drink of the Bays' water,
    You children of an Ass?"

"Why shouldn't we muddy your water?
    Neigh! neigh! neigh!
Why shouldn't we drink of your water,
    Pray, pray, pray?
If our Sire was a Coster's Donkey
    Our Dam was a Golden Bay,
And the Mules shall drink of the Bays' water
    Every other day!"

Jack Straw's Castle

JACK STRAW
    Laid down the Law
And vowed there was nothing for building like
    Straw.
He built him a Castle in less than a day,
Its Walls were of Stubble, its Roof was of Hay.
A capful of wind flew out of the shaw
And blew down his Castle, and blew up Jack
    Straw!

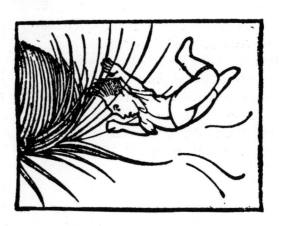

Marylebone

MARY LEBONE
    She gets no meat,
She never has anything
Nice to eat;
A supper fit
For a dog alone
Is all the fare
Of poor Mary Lebone.
She squats by the corner
Of Baker Street,
And snuffs at the air
So spicy and sweet
When the Bakers are baking
The puddings and pies,
Their buns and their biscuits
And Banburies—
A tart for Joscelyn,
A cake for Joan,
And nothing at all
For poor Mary Lebone!

Snowfields and Blackwall

THE Snow is on the Snow-fields,
　　The Soot is on the Wall—
A black Wall, a white Field,
　　And that's all.

Serpentine

SERPENTINE this way, serpentine that,
    The way the Serpent went after the Rat—
The Rat jumped into the Round Pond,
But the Serpent didn't mind *that:*
The Rat ran into the Bird-cage,
And now the Serpent's fat!

Bugsby's Reach

BUGSBY'S reach is long as time,
    His reach as wide as wind is,
He can pick you nettles in Greenwich Marsh
    And docks in the East Indies.

Cherry Gardens

WHERE d'ye buy your ear-rings,
  Your pretty bobbing ear-rings,
Where d'ye buy your ear-rings,
  Moll and Sue and Nan?—
In the Cherry Gardens
They sell 'em eight a penny,
And let you eat as many
  As ever you can!

Moll's are ruddy coral,
Sue's are glossy jet,
Nan's are yellow ivory,
  Swinging on their stems.
O you lucky damsels
To get in Cherry Gardens
Ear-rings for your fardens
  Comelier than gems.

The World's End

A COACH-AND-SIX to Chelsea,
   A coach-and-six to Chelsea,
A coach-and-six to Chelsea,
   Trying to reach the World's End!

All the world was there a-walking,
Running, riding, tripping, stalking,
Singing, dancing, laughing, talking,
   Trying to reach the World's End.

Lords and ladies, carters, reapers,
Maids-in-waiting, poachers, keepers,
Chamberlains and chimney-sweepers,
   Trying to reach the World's End.

'Prentices and bonnet-makers,
Children, Aldermen, Jews and Quakers,
Grenadiers and undertakers,
   Trying to reach the World's End.

A coach-and-six to Chelsea,
A coach-and-six to Chelsea,
A coach-and-six to Chelsea,
   Trying to reach the World's End!

Newington Butts

THE bung is lost from Newington Butts!
  The beer is running in all the ruts,
The gutters are swimming, the Butts are dry
Lackadaisy! and so am I.
Who was the thief that stole the bung?
I shall go hopping the day he's hung!

London Fields

PRETTY, go walk in London Fields
  With lad's-love in your shoe,
And the first you meet in London Fields
  Will be the lad for you.

Perhaps he'll bear a gilded mace,
  Perhaps he'll wear a sword,
Perhaps he'll be a lamplighter,
  Perhaps he'll be a lord.

O if among the throng to-day
  You'd meet your love so true,
Pretty, go walk in London Fields
  With lad's-love in your shoe.

Kew

K EW is for Flowers, Red, Yellow and Blue;
When the Flowers are in Bloom, You and
I are for Kew.

The Treasury

IF I had all the silver and gold
In the King's Treasury, in the King's
Treasury,
D'ye think I'd cry Crumpets out here in the
cold?
I'd sit by the fireside until I grew old,
If I had all the silver and gold
In the King's Treasury, in the King's Treasury.

If I had all the diamonds and pearls
In the Queen's Treasury, in the Queen's
Treasury,
D'ye think I'd hawk laces for other young
girls?
I'd buy a green jewel to hang in my curls,
If I had all the diamonds and pearls
In the Queen's Treasury, in the Queen's
Treasury.

Scotland Yard

How long's the Yard in Scotland?
   Tell me that now, Mother."
"Six-and-thirty inches, Daughter,
   Just like any other."
"O isn't it thirty-five, Mother?"
   "No more than thirty-seven."
"Then the bonnie lad that sold me plaid
   Will never get to Heaven!"

Goose Green

WHEN I came to London my fortune to seek
  I was hired to the Goose-Green for two-
    pence a week.

With one grey Gander and twelve white Geese
And twenty brown Goslings there isn't much
  peace.

If I try to say Bo! I can't hear myself speak,
But I live by the Goose-Green on twopence a
  week.

The Geese and the Gander they gobble the grass,
And I shan't be happy till Michaelmas.

I want to trudge home but I haven't the cheek,
For I came to London my fortune to seek,
So I sit on the Goose-Green at twopence a week.

Cornhill

THE seed of the corn, the rustling corn,
  The seed of the corn is sown,
When the seed is sown on the Corn-hill
  My love will ask for his own.

The blade of the corn, the rustling corn,
  The blade of the corn is shown;
When the blade is shown on the Corn-hill
  I'll promise my love his own.

The ear of the corn, the rustling corn,
  The ear of the corn is grown;
When the ear is grown on the Corn-hill
  My love shall have his own.

The sheaf of the corn, the rustling corn.
  The sheaf of the corn is mown;
When the sheaf is mown on the Corn-hil!
  My love will leave his own.

Brick Lane

SAID This Fool to That Fool when April did
fall,
"How many leaves, Fool, to build a green wall?"
Said That Fool to This in the sun and the rain,
"As many as bricks, Fool, to plant a brick lane."

Marble Arch

A MARBLE Arch for Heroes
    To walk in,
    To walk in,
A Red-Rose Arch for Ladies
    To talk in,
    To talk in,
A Hempen Arch for Little Girls
    To skip in,
    To skip in,
An Arch of Stars for
      Babies
    To sleep in,
    To sleep in.

Shoreditch

O THE water,
  The rolling water,
The deep sea-water on every hand!
From the end of the world and it may be further
The tide doth glide to drink the land.
  A shore-ditch, a shore-ditch,
  A bottomless shore-ditch!
A ditch, dig a ditch the length of the shore,
To swallow the water, the rolling water,
Or the town will drown for evermore!

Maiden Lane and Swain's Lane

THE Maiden is crying in *her* lane,
    And the Swain is sighing in *his*,
And neither the Swain nor the Maiden
    Will say what the matter is.
But if the Swain went into *her* lane,
    Or the Maiden went into the Swain's,
'There'd soon be an end of the crying and sighing
    In both those lanes.

Old Bailey

I STOLE a duck from the old Baily's yard,
   The duck she said Quack! and the Baily ran
      hard;
The Baily ran hard, but still harder ran I—
If he'd been a *young* Baily, duckling, good-bye!

The Welsh Harp

O MY harp, my tuneful harp,
  It sang so sweet and clearly!
O my harp, my pretty harp,
  I loved my Welsh harp dearly.

My harp and I a-wandering
  Went over Snowdon Mountain,
From Anglesey to Swansea Bay
  It sang like any fountain.

Now was not I a silly lad
  To pine for London City?
My harp fell silent on the road
  And would not sing a ditty.

By Collin Dale and Watling Street
  I went, my heart a-sinking,
And now my harp lies in the Brent,
  It dropped while I was drinking.

4

O my harp, my tuneful harp,
  That sang in Wales so pretty!
I sit and mourn my lost Welsh harp,
  What care I for the city?

St. Mary Axe

SAINT MARY, ax, Saint Mary, ax,
  Saint Mary, ax your fill,
Saint Mary, ax whatever you lacks
  And you shall have your will.—
O bring me a Rose, a Christmas Rose
  To climb my window-sill.—
You shall have your Rose when Heaven snows,
  Saint Mary, sleep until.

Westminster

INSIDE the West Minster
   As the sun went down
I heard a white-robed Angel
Sing for London Town.

Outside the West Minster
When the sky was red
I saw a ragged Choir-boy
Slip home to bed.

Kilburn

KILL, kill, kill!
    Cries the Black Plague of London.
  Burn, burn, burn!
Cries the Great Fire of London.
    Kill, kill, kill!
    London's very ill.
    Burn, burn, burn!
    London takes a turn.
Kill! Burn! Kill! Burn!
    Burn the Plague out—
London will get well again,
    There isn't any doubt.

Gospel Oak and
Honor Oak

KING CHARLES he sat up an Oak-tree,
  But it wasn't the Gospel Oak,
For King Charles said more than his Gospel,
  And winked as soon as he'd spoke.

King Charles he sat up an Oak-tree,
  But it wasn't the Honor Oak,
For King Charles was so nice of his honour
  That he kept it under a cloak.

Little Britain

SAYS Big Spain
    To Little Britain,
"I'm the Dog
And you're the Kitten!
So haul in your sheet
And call in your Fleet,
Or you'll get bitten,
Little Britain!"

To Big Spain
Says Little Britain,
"Dogs will run
When Cats start spitting."
She chased Big Spain
Across the Main—
"Who got bitten?"
Says Little Britain.

The Grove

ON the high road to Richmond,
   All in the Grove,
I heard a White Blackbird
   Sing for his love :
He sang so brightly,
He sang so lightly,
He sang so sprightly,
   All in the Grove !
Lilli-loo-loo-loo ! lilli-loo-loo-loo !
  All down the Richmond Road—
Lilli-loo-loo-loo ! lilli-loo-loo-loo !
  All in the Grove.

Nag's Head

"You hold the Nag's head
    While I go in;
If you hold the Nag's head
    I'll get a pot o' gin."
"Nay, *you* hold the Nag's head
    Till I come out;
If you hold the Nag's head
    I'll get a mug o' stout."
"You want stout,
    I want gin—
Let the Nag have her head,
    We'll both go in!"

Lavender Hill

LAUNDRYMAID, whither?—Up Lavender Hill
    With a pocket of dimity bags to fill
For bolster and coverlet, pillow and sheet,
To keep the linen smelling sweet.
   I'll lay them up in lavender,
   I'll lay them up in lavender,
   I'll lay them up in lavender,
     And you'll sleep sweet.

Laundrymaid, linger! the sun's so hot!
Sit with me on a shady plot
And promise come Sunday to be my wife,
For I love you better than I love life.
   And I'll lay you up in lavender,
   I'll lay you up in lavender,
   I'll lay you up in lavender
     The rest of your life.

Mile End

How far to the mile end?—
   Never ask me!
It may be less than five mile,
   It must be more than three.
If I catch the old man
   That led me astray,
I'll thrash him with a tape-measure
   The whole of the way.

Blackheath

THE Witch of the Heath flew up to the Moon
  To sweep the Old Man's chimney down;
The pitch fell out of the sky like rain,
And the black Heath will never be green again.

The Tower

THEY put a Lady in the Tower,
    Heigh-O, fiddlededee!
They put a Lady in the Tower
And told her she was in their power,
And left her there for half an hour,
    Heigh-O, fiddlededee!

They put a Padlock on the Chain,
    Heigh-O, fiddlededee!
They put a Padlock on the Chain,
But they left the Key in the South of Spain,
So the Lady took it off again,
    Heigh-O, fiddlededee!

They put a Bulldog at the Door,
    Heigh-O, fiddlededee!
They put a Bulldog at the Door,
He was so old he could only snore,
And he'd lost his Tooth the day before,
    Heigh-O, fiddlededee!

They put a Beefeater at the Gate,
    Heigh-O, fiddlededee!

They put a Beefeater at the Gate,
But as his age was eighty-eight
His Grandmother said he couldn't wait,
    Heigh-O, fiddlededee!

They put a Prince to watch the Stair,
    Heigh-O, fiddlededee!
They put a Prince to watch the Stair,
But he had a Golden Ring to spare,
So he married the Lady then and there,
    Heigh-O, fiddlededee!

And ever since that grievous hour,
    Heigh-O, fiddlededee!
Ever since that grievous hour
When the lovely Lady was in their power
They've never put nobody in the Tower,
    Heigh-O, fiddlededee!

Bevis Marks

Bevis marks the blackboard, Bevis marks his
    socks,
Bevis marks the time o' day by the City clocks;
Even if a pin drops Bevis says, "Hark !"
There's nothing worth mentioning that Bevis
    doesn't mark.

Bow

MILLY has a blue bow,
  Willy has a yew-bow,
Which is the better bow?
  I don't know!
I'll borrow Milly's bow when I go to Chapel,
And I'll borrow Willy's when I want to shoot
  an apple.

Moorgate

WHEN I was small I ran away
    And through the Moor-gate tried to stray
  To pick a bunch of heather ;
But there a man paced to and fro
In garments that were white as snow,
  Though he was brown as leather.

His sword was like the sickle
    moon,
He stood up in his scarlet
    shoon
    Taller than any other !
He laid his finger on his
    breast,
And he looked East, so I
    ran West
    Crying for my Mother.

The Garden City

I HAD a pretty Garden
   Full of blowing flowers,
Singing-birds and honey-bees
And fountains throwing showers.
Up came Jerry,
Whom I'll never, never pardon,
And when I wasn't looking
Built a city in my Garden.
Out upon you, Jerry! Jerry, you're a pity!
Jerry, turn about and plant a garden in the City!

Willesden

I went into Will's Den
    To sweep and scour and swill;
Will scowled through his spectacles
    And took it very ill.
"I'm come to turn out your Den, Will"—
    "Turn yourself out!" says Will.

Friday Street

WHERE shall we meet, O where shall we
meet?
We'll meet to be sure in Friday Street.

Shall we meet on Saturday?—O dear no!
On Saturday, on Saturday I have to knead the
dough.

Shall we meet on Sunday?—O dear no!
On Sunday, on Sunday to church I must go.

Shall we meet on Monday?—O dear no!
On Monday I wash linen as white as driven snow.

Shall we meet on Tuesday?—O dear no!
On Tuesday I darn the socks, heel and toe.

Shall we meet on Wednesday?—O dear no!
On Wednesday I've a meadowful of grass to
mow.

Shall we meet on Thursday?—O dear no!
On Thursday my best bonnet wants a new satin
bow.

Then when shall we meet, O when shall we meet?
On Friday to be sure in Friday Street.

Hackney

QUICK, quick!
A Hackney Wick!
The Beadle and Mayor in the marsh do stick.
The coachman ups
And the hackney downs,
And the Mayor and the Beadle have bumped
their crowns!

Millwall

I LEANED on the Mill-Wall
   Looking at the water,
I leaned on the Mill-Wall
   And saw the Nis's Daughter.

I saw the Nis's Daughter
   Playing with her ball,
She tossed it and tossed it
   Against the Mill-Wall.

I saw the Nis's Goodwife
   Busy making lace
With her silver bobbins
   In the Mill-Race.

Then I saw the Old Nis,
   His hair to his heel,
Combing out the tangles
   On the Mill-Wheel.

The Miller came behind me
   And gave my ear a clout—
"Get on with your business,
   You good-for-nothing lout!"

Haberdashers' Row

NINE-AND-NINETY Haberdashers all in a row!
  Where did the Hundredth Haberdasher
    go?
He ran to fetch a pin for the Wife of the Beadle,
And he couldn't find her anything but Cleo-
    patra's Needle.
All over London he's dashing to and fro,
And there's none to fill his gap in the Haber-
    dashers' row.

Kentish Town

As I jogged by a Kentish Town
  Delighting in the crops,
I met a gypsy hazel-brown
  With a basketful of hops.

"You Sailor from the Dover Coast
  With your blue eyes full of ships,
Carry my basket to the oast
  And I'll kiss you on the lips."

Once she kissed me with a jest,
  Once with a tear—
O where's the heart was in my breast,
  And the ring was in my ear?

The Caledonian Market

I AM going tae the Caledonian Market, my ain
    lass,
  An' I'll bring ye back some trifles for a
    fairing—
O, the Stone of Scone I'll bring for your pretty
    finger-ring,
  An' the silk o' Bruce's Spider for your
    wearing.
Ye shall ha'e the broken dirk Wallace brandished
    at Falkirk,
  An' a lovelock from the beid o' Bonnie
    Charlie—
O I'll bring ye, my ain lass, Mary Stewart's
    looking-glass,
  Gin ye'll meet me when I'm coming through
    the barley.

Kingsland

What's King's Land?
  What's King's Land?
  Here where I stand,
  That's King's Land!
With Islington to west of me,
Canonbury abreast of me,
With Hackney to the East of me,
And Dalston not the least of me,
With Stamford to the North of me,
And Stoke gone forth of me,
With Shoreditch to the South of me,
And London at the mouth of me—
    That's King's Land,
    Here where I stand,
    And none shall win a hand
    Of all the King's Land!

Saint Paul's Churchyard

Whom first shall we lay in Saint Paul's
    Churchyard?
Whom first shall we lay in Saint Paul's Church-
    yard?
    The Smith and his Hound
    We will lay in the ground,
May their bodies sleep sound in Saint Paul's
    Churchyard.

Whom next shall we lay in Saint Paul's Church-
    yard?
Whom next shall we lay in Saint Paul's Church-
    yard?
    The Blackfriars, the Whitefriars,
    The Clerks and the Canons,
And the Knights with their pennons shall lie in
    the Yard.

Whom third shall we lay in Saint Paul's Church-
    yard?
Whom third shall we lay in Saint Paul's Church-
    yard?
    Big Ben, Gog and Magog,
    Old Ford and Old Bailey,
And may they dream gaily in Paul's Churchyard.

Whom fourth shall we lay in Saint Paul's
    Churchyard?
Whom fourth shall we lay in Saint Paul's
    Churchyard?

The Lion, the Unicorn,
George and the Dragon,
Shall give over wrangling and lie in the Yard.

Whom fifth shall we lay in Saint Paul's Church-
yard?
Whom fifth shall we lay in Saint Paul's Church-
yard?
Punch, Judy, and Toby
Alongside their Showman,
Jack Straw and Piers Plowman shall lie in the
Yard.

Whom sixth shall we lay in Saint Paul's Church-
yard?
Whom sixth shall we lay in Saint Paul's Church-
yard?
The Muffin-and-Crumpet-Man,
Jack-in-the-Green,
And the little May-Queen shall all lie in the
Yard.

Whom last shall we lay in Saint Paul's Church-
yard?
Whom last shall we lay in Saint Paul's Church-
yard?
We will lay there Dick Whittington,
Lord Mayor of London,
While the bells ring at sundown in Paul's
Churchyard.